For Milo, whose idea it was
—D.S.

For my dear Mela and her little
princess Maya, thanks a lot for all!
—V.D.

DIAL BOOKS FOR YOUNG READERS
A division of Penguin Young Readers Group
New York, NY 10014, U.S.A.
Penguin Group (Canada), 90 Eglinton Avenue East, Suite 700,
Toronto, Ontario, Canada M4P 2Y3
(a division of Pearson Penguin Canada Inc.)
Penguin Books Ltd, 80 Strand,
London WC2R 0RL, England
Penguin Ireland, 25 St. Stephen's Green, Dublin 2, Ireland
(a division of Penguin Books Ltd)
Penguin Group (Australia), 250 Camberwell Road,
Camberwell, Victoria 3124, Australia
(a division of Pearson Australia Group Pty Ltd)
Penguin Books India Pvt Ltd, 11 Community Centre,
Panchsheel Park, New Delhi - 110 017, India
Penguin Group (NZ), 67 Apollo Drive, Rosedale, Auckland
0632, New Zealand (a division of Pearson New Zealand Ltd)
Penguin Books (South Africa) (Pty) Ltd, 24 Sturdee Avenue,
Rosebank, Johannesburg 2196, South Africa
Penguin Books Ltd, Registered Offices: 80 Strand,
London WC2R 0RL, England

Text copyright © 2012 by Dashka Slater
Pictures copyright © 2012 by Valeria Docampo

Designed by Jasmin Rubero
Text set in Celestia Antigua Std
Manufactured in China on acid-free paper.

10 9 8 7 6 5 4 3 2

Library of Congress Cataloging-in-Publication Data
is available upon request

Dangerously Ever After

by Dashka Slater

illustrated by Valeria Docampo

Dial Books for Young Readers
an imprint of Penguin Group (USA) Inc.

Princess Amanita loved things that were dangerous. She loved her pet scorpion, and her brakeless bicycle, and her collection of daggers and broken glass. She loved leaning out of the topmost turret in the castle, and walking blindfolded at the edge of the moat. But most of all she loved her garden, which was said to be the most dangerous in the world.

Princess Amanita's garden was filled with prickles and stickles and brambles and nettles. There were plants that stung, and plants that stunk, and plants with spikes so sharp that the palace gardeners wore armor when they weeded them.

One day, as the princess was watering a patch of itching thistles, a prince from a neighboring kingdom rode up. His name was Florian and he was out looking for a dragon to slay, or a knight to challenge—or at least someone his own age to talk to.

"Hello," he said. "Nice flowers."

"They're not at all nice," said Amanita. "Their itch is worse than a thousand mosquito bites."

Then she noticed the prince's sword, which looked very sharp and dangerous. "Nice sword," she remarked.

Prince Florian took the sword from his belt and waved it in the air. "See that bunch of grapes?"

"Those aren't grapes," Amanita started to say. "They're—"

But it was too late. Florian had already sliced them from the vine.

Unfortunately, they were grenapes, which explode three seconds after being picked. They landed in the princess's brand-new ruby-studded wheelbarrow and blew a large hole in the bottom.

"Oops," Prince Florian said.

Princess Amanita just stared at him with her hands on her hips until he got back on his bicycle and rode away.

The next day, Prince Florian arrived at the palace with a large bunch of pink roses. "I'm really sorry about the wheelbarrow," he said. "But since you like flowers, I thought you might like these."

The princess looked at the flowers curiously. "What are they?" she asked.

"They're roses. My kingdom is famous for them."

"But what do they do?"

Prince Florian was puzzled. "Do?"

"Are their leaves as sharp as razors?" Amanita prompted. "Do they stink worse than a giant's armpit? Do they climb up the roof and pull off the shingles?"

"They… uh… smell nice," Prince Florian answered at last. "And they're … pretty."

"Oh," said the princess, and rolled her eyes.

She was about to toss the roses in the trash when something sharp pierced her palm. She took a closer look. Lining each stem were thorns as long and as sharp as sharks' teeth.

"What did you say these were called?" she asked the prince.

"Roses."

"They're wonderful," Amanita said, and immediately plunged them in a vase—stem side up, naturally.

Feeling a little friendlier, Princess Amanita invited the prince for a walk through her garden. She showed him the heckle-berries, which shouted insults at him as he passed . . .

. . . the swinging mace vine, which nearly took his head off . . .

. . . and the stink lilies, which smelled like a mixture of dog food, cabbage, and Limburger cheese.

"I would love to grow some of those dangerous flowers you brought," the princess said at last. "Do you think you could send me some seeds?"

Prince Florian hesitated. He was very familiar with the royal stables, and the royal library, and the shelf in the royal kitchen where the cookies were kept, but he had never spent much time in the royal garden before gathering roses for the princess that morning.

Princess Amanita made an exasperated face. "Just give this note to your gardener," she said. Using a pen she'd made out of a six-inch cactus spine, she scribbled a message on a piece of royal stationery. It said:

The princess was overjoyed when the package of nine seeds arrived. She planted them outside her bedroom window and watched eagerly as they sprouted and grew. At last the new plants bloomed. But instead of thorny pink roses, each one blossomed into a large pink nose.

Almost immediately, the nine noses began to sniff. Then they began to twitch. And finally, they began to sneeze.

"Bless you!" said Princess Amanita. "Bless you! Bless you! Bless you! Bless you! Bless you! Bless you! Bless—oh, never mind."

The noses, it seemed, were allergic to every other plant in the garden. They sneezed all morning and all afternoon. By evening, the sneezes had blown the needles off the cactuses and covered the garden with sticky goo.

That night, the noses began to snore. It sounded like a troop of monkeys playing tubas. No one in the palace got a wink of sleep.

When morning came, Princess Amanita marched outside and pulled up each of the noses by the roots. Then she climbed onto her brakeless bicycle. "I'm going to find Prince Florian, and when I do, I'm going to stick these noses in his ear," she announced as she rode off.

The princess sped pell-mell down one gigantic hill after another, turning left or right as the mood struck her…

Until she found herself riding through a dark, gloomy forest. Suddenly she realized she didn't have the faintest idea where Prince Florian lived. Come to think of it, she didn't have any idea how to get back home either. In fact, she was lost.

She stopped pedaling. A howl echoed through the trees that might have been the wind, but might also have been a large, hungry, princess-eating wolf.

"This place seems kind of dangerous," Princess Amanita said to the noses. "Of course, I love dangerous things." She looked around. "I love sharp-toothed goblins, and carnivorous spiders, and the witch that probably lives in that cottage, and being lost in the forest all by myself."

By the time she got to the end of the sentence, Amanita knew that she wasn't exactly telling the truth.

She did love dangerous things. She just loved them a lot more when she was safe at home in the palace.

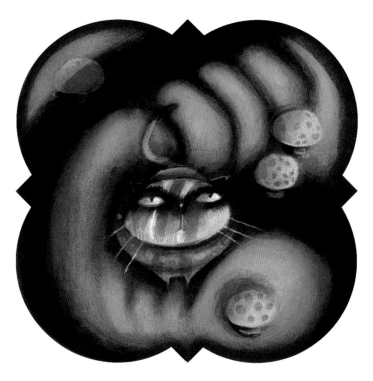

"It's all your fault!" Amanita told the noses. "How am I going to find Prince Florian? All I know about him is that he has a garden filled with roses."

The noses sniffed sympathetically, as if they too were on the verge of tears. Then they sniffed some more.

"I wish you would stop that horrible snuffling," scolded the princess. "You sound like a herd of warthogs."

But when she looked at the noses, she saw that all nine were pointing in the same direction and sniffing so hard it seemed they might fall off their stems.

"I wonder what you smell," Princess Amanita said thoughtfully. "Maybe it's dinner."

Hoping that it was, as it had been a very long time since lunch, the princess began pedaling in the direction the noses were pointing.

The noses sniffed and snorted, and after a while the princess began sniffing too.

She smelled something wonderful.

It smelled like candy and lemons and cloves.

It smelled like sleeping in the sun and staying up late for a party.

It smelled like secrets and summer and beautiful dresses and the kind of folding knife that comes with scissors and a screwdriver.

It was the smell of thousands of roses.

And there, on the horizon, was Prince Florian's castle.

When Princess Amanita saw Prince Florian, she didn't feel like sticking the noses in his ear anymore, so she gave them to him as a bouquet.

"What do they do?" he asked.

"They smell good," the princess said. "I mean, they smell well. Anyway, they're good at smelling."

After dinner, the prince took Princess Amanita to see the royal rose garden. The noses came too, sniffing happily. They didn't sneeze once.

"Maybe we could plant them here," suggested Princess Amanita.

And so they did. The roses didn't mind the noses, and the noses loved the roses. Both, in fact, lived happily ever after.

As for Princess Amanita, she went home with nine
of the thorniest rosebushes in the royal garden.
They were just as dangerous as she had hoped.
And they smelled nice too.